Dear Parent:
Your child's love of reading s

Every child learns to read in a different way and at his or her own speed. You can help your young reader improve and become more confident by encouraging his or her own interests and abilities. You can also guide your child's spiritual development by reading stories with biblical values and Bible stories, like I Can Read! books published by Zonderkidz. From books your child reads with you to the first books he or she reads alone, there are I Can Read! books for every stage of reading:

SHARED READING
Basic language, word repetition, and whimsical illustrations, ideal for sharing with your emergent reader.

BEGINNING READING
Short sentences, familiar words, and simple concepts for children eager to read on their own.

READING WITH HELP
Engaging stories, longer sentences, and language play for developing readers.

READING ALONE
Complex plots, challenging vocabulary, and high-interest topics for the independent reader.

ADVANCED READING
Short paragraphs, chapters, and exciting themes for the perfect bridge to chapter books.

I Can Read! books have introduced children to the joy of reading since 1957. Featuring award-winning authors and illustrators and a fabulous cast of beloved characters, I Can Read! books set the standard for beginning readers.

A lifetime of discovery begins with the magical words **"I Can Read!"**

Visit www.icanread.com for information on enriching your child's reading experience.
Visit www.zonderkidz.com for more Zonderkidz I Can Read! titles.

The Lord gives wisdom. Knowledge and understanding come from his mouth.
—Proverbs 2:6

www.zonderkidz.com

Super Ace and the Mega Wow 3000

Requests for information should be addressed to:
Zonderkidz, *Grand Rapids, Michigan 49530*

Library of Congress Cataloging-in-Publication Data

Crouch, Cheryl, 1968-
Super Ace and the Mega Wow 3000 / story by Cheryl Crouch ; pictures by Matt Vander Pol.
p. cm. -- (I can read! Level 2)
ISBN 978-0-310-71696-9 (softcover)
[1. Superheroes--Fiction. 2. Christian life--Fiction.] I. Vander Pol, Matt, 1972- ill. II. Title.
PZ7.C8838St 2009
[E]--dc22 2008038574

Art Direction & Design: Jody Langley

Printed in China

09 10 11 12 • 4 3 2 1

story by Cheryl Crouch

pictures by Matt Vander Pol

Super Ace and Sidekick Ned
flew through deep, dark space.

BEEP! BEEP! BEEP!

"It's my super phone.

Someone on Planet Floop needs help!"

said Super Ace.

Flooper met them on Floop.

"Super Ace! I am glad to see you!"

Super Ace stood big and tall.

"Yes, you are glad to see me."

Flooper did not talk to Ned.

Ned was just a sidekick.

Super Ace said, “How can I help?”

Flooper pointed. “See my spaceship?

It is a Mega Wow 3000.”

Ned smiled and said, “Cool ship!”

Super Ace did not smile.
“Did you call to show me your ship?
It is a good spaceship,
but my jet pack
is faster than a Mega Wow 3000.”
Flooper’s face turned red.

“This ship is full of food
for hungry kids,” said Flooper.
Ned smiled and said, “How nice!”
Super Ace did not smile.

"Did you call to tell me
that you did something good?
I do very good, important things
all the time."

Flooper's face got even redder.
He said, "Super Ace,
the ship will not go.
I need your help!"

Super Ace smiled. “I can help.

I am a superhero.

I have two superpowers.”

He made fists. “I am super strong.”

He fluffed his hair. “I look good.”

“Is that a superpower?”

asked Flooper.

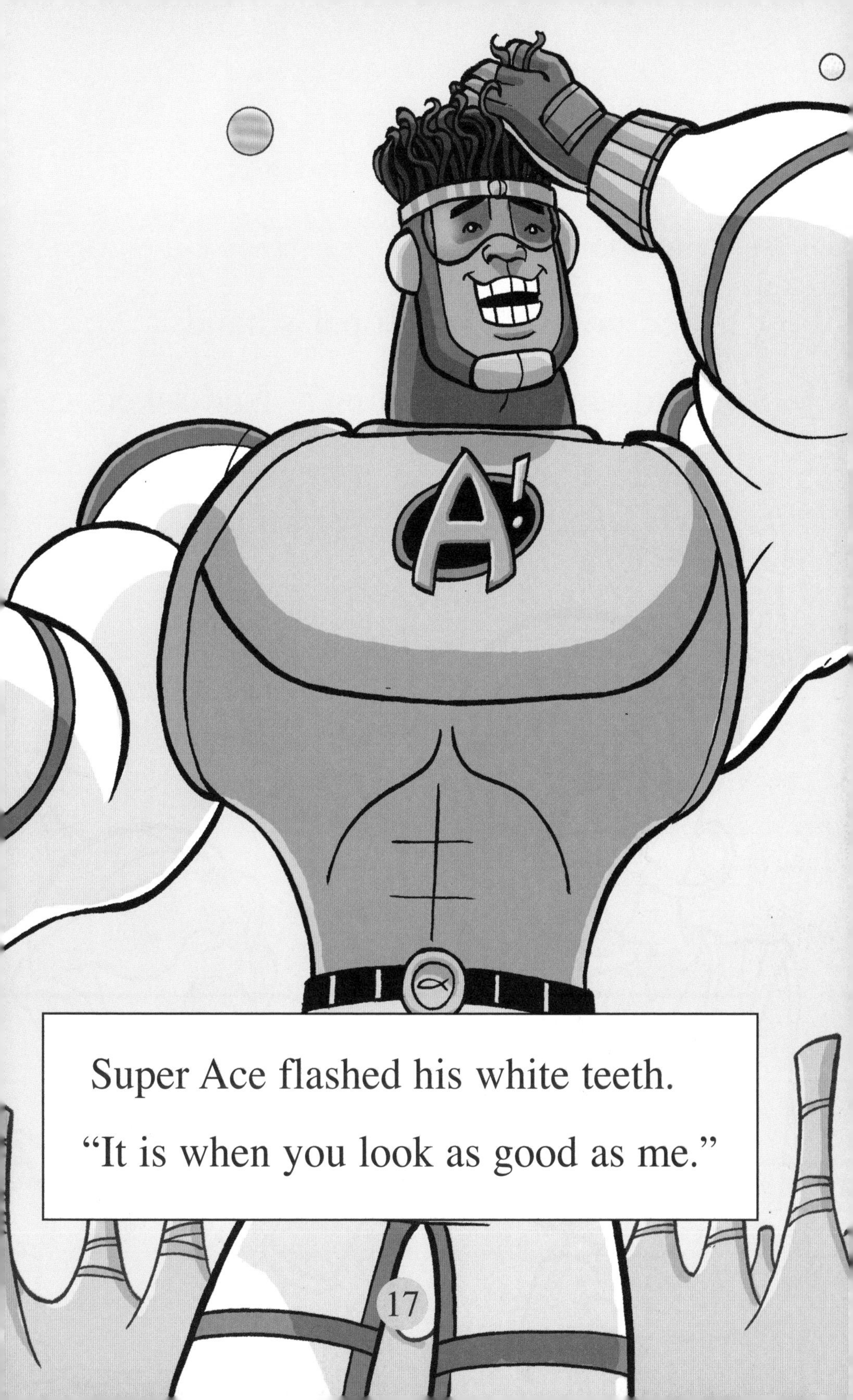

Super Ace flashed his white teeth.

"It is when you look as good as me."

“Can your powers help fix my ship?” Flooper asked.

Ned pointed to Flooper’s hand.

“Did you try that thing?” Ned asked.

Super Ace frowned.

"Ned, you are a sidekick.

You can stand beside me,

but I will fix the ship.

I do not need your help."

Ned stood by him.

Super Ace said,
“I lift with my big arms.”
He lifted the hood.
The hood came off!
Super Ace said,
“I bend with my big arms.”
He bent things
inside the Mega Wow 3000.

Super Ace said,

"I move stuff with my big arms."

He picked up the Mega Wow 3000.

"See? Your ship will not go,

so I will carry it to the kids."

Flooper said, "It is a long way."

Super Ace said, "I can do it."

MW 3000

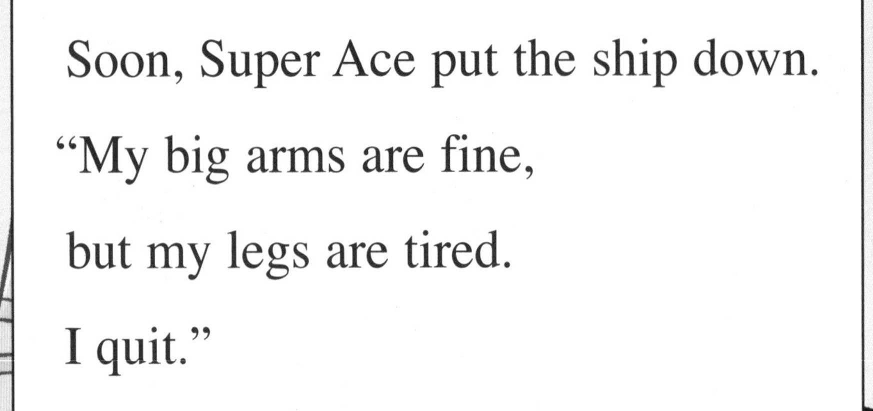

Soon, Super Ace put the ship down.

"My big arms are fine,

but my legs are tired.

I quit."

"Well, can you use your good looks
to fix my ship?" asked Flooper.
Super Ace shook his head.
"My looks are just to look at."

Flooper turned to Sidekick Ned.

"What is your superpower, Ned?"

Super Ace laughed.

“His superpower is wisdom.

Ha! You cannot even see wisdom.”

“Ned, can you use your superpower

to fix my ship?” asked Flooper.

Ned said, “Maybe.
I think the thing
in your hand is a key.
Try it.”

Flooper put the key in the keyhole.

He turned it, and the ship started.

"Now I can feed the kids.

Thank you, Ned!" said Flooper.

Ned folded his hands to pray.

“Let’s thank God,” Ned said.

“And me!” said Super Ace.
He puffed out his chest.
“Now we must go help others.”
Sidekick Ned nodded at Flooper,
and Flooper smiled at Ned.

Then Super Ace and Sidekick Ned flew back into deep, dark space.